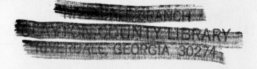

To Betsy Hass

First Edition · Copyright © 1982 by Ezra Jack Keats · All rights reserved · First published in 1982 by The Viking Press, 625 Madison Avenue, New York, New York 10022 · Published simultaneously in Canada by Penguin Books Canada Limited · Printed in U.S.A.
1 2 3 4 5 86 85 84 83 82

Library of Congress Cataloging in Publication Data
Keats, Ezra Jack.   Clementina's cactus.
Summary: Clementina discovers a delightful surprise deep inside the prickly skin of the cactus.   [1. Cactus—Fiction. 2. Stories without words] I. Title.
PZ7.K2253CL   [Fic]   82-2630   ISBN 0-670-22517-7   AACR2

CLEMENTINA'S CACTUS

EZRA JACK KEATS

The Viking Press New York